NORTH AMERICAN INDIAN STORIES

More Star Tales

398.2 May MS

Retold and Illustrated by
Gretchen Will Mayo

WALKER AND COMPANY
NEW YORK

Published simultaneously in Canada by
Thomas Allen & Son Canada, Limited, Markham, Ontario.

Book design by Laurie McBarnette

Library of Congress Cataloging-in-Publication Data

Mayo, Gretchen Will.
More star tales : North American Indian stories / by Gretchen Will Mayo. — 1st pbk. ed.
p.   cm.
Includes bibliographical references.
Summary: A collection of Indian legends about the stars, moon, and nighttime sky.
ISBN 0-8027-7347-8 (pbk.)
1. Indians of North America—Legends. 2. Stars—Folklore.
3. Moon—Folklore. [1. Indians of North America—Legends.
2. Stars—Folklore. 3. Moon—Folklore.] I. Title.
E98.F6M347   1990
398.26—dc20
[398.2]
[E]   90-12786
CIP
LC

Printed in the United States of America

Originally published in hardcover in 1987 by the Walker Publishing Company, Inc.

2   4   6   8   10   9   7   5   3   1

For Tom,
Meg, Molly and Ann

**My appreciation and thanks
to Dr. Alice B. Kehoe
and
the Milwaukee Public Museum**

CONTENTS

INTRODUCTION

Leaning close to a glowing campfire, a gathering of young people watch The Old One as he acts out a story. His wrinkled hands stroke the night air. He is describing Crane Woman's escape from her earthly husband, the greedy and evil Wolf Man. Crane Woman and her two starving sons have nowhere else to run from the wicked Wolf Man, but they find safety in the sky where they will become stars.

The young people are Native American Indians. The stories might have been told last night or a hundred years ago, for the tale of Crane Woman is an ancient one. Native American Indians have spun tales for one another for century upon century. Their stories reflect their ways of life, their beliefs, and the laws of their tribes.

Some of the storytellers were farmers. They told tales of Corn Maiden. Other Indians roamed the plains, hunting buffalo. From their tribes came stories of ghostly buffalo herds. There were whalers and salmon fishermen, trappers and shepherds, basket weavers and potters. The countless ancient Indian tribes were as different as the land was different across the continent, but they all shared a love for storytelling.

Native American ancestors were keenly aware of the land and the sky that surrounded them. They felt that all creation was connected. They believed that spirits could appear in all things, from rocks to ravens to falling stars. When they looked at the night sky, they joined all the world's people in imagining what the stars could be. They wove many tales about the sky country.

The gifted Indian tale-spinners have passed along the thread of their Native American stories from generation to generation. Sometimes they have reverently conformed to the original myths. Often they embellished the tales with details springing from their own imaginations. The stories in this collection are another link in that creative storytelling tradition and are offered with a sense of appreciation for what has been told before.

MORE STAR TALES

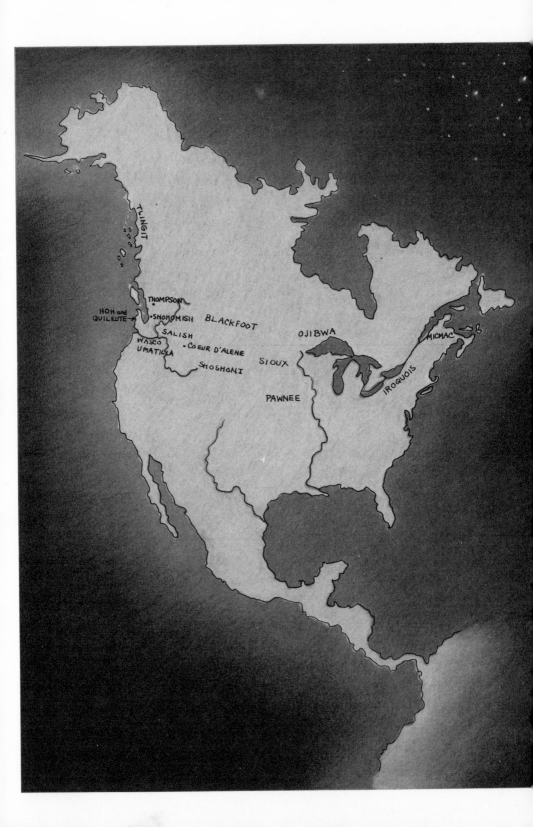

The Never-Ending Bear Hunt

The stars in the sky seem to revolve around the North Star, also called Polaris, during the night. The sky appears to change as the night moves on, but it also changes throughout the year. The two constellations of Bootes and Corona Borealis seem to sink so low in the night sky that they disappear below the horizon and aren't seen for several months of the year. At the same time, the Big Dipper is visible all year long but looks like it is standing upright during some months and upside down in others. Stars don't really move, but they appear to because the earth spins on its axis.

The Micmac Indians of Nova Scotia told a story to fit the changing look of the starry sky. It is a story that never ends.

THE NEVER-ENDING BEAR HUNT

The Big Dipper
Bootes
Corona Borealis

Far away in the sky country, a bear woke up from a long winter sleep. She left her rocky den on the hill and lumbered off to search for berries. A sharp-eyed chickadee, flitting around the bushes, saw the bear and flew off to call his friends around him.

"It has been a long winter and I am hungry," said Chickadee. "I am going bear hunting. Who will come with me?"

Six of his friends agreed to join Chickadee, and at once they set out to find the bear.

Chickadee was the smallest hunter, but he was also the wisest. He carried along a pot for boiling his dinner. Robin, who was larger, was called upon to lead the hunting party. Moose-bird was impatient and took his place behind Chickadee. He intended to help himself to Chickadee's pot. Pigeon, Blue Jay, Horned Owl and Saw-whet all fell into place behind Moose-bird as the party started out.

Since food had been scarce through the winter, the hunters hurried to track their dinner. They found, though, that large and awkward as she seemed, Bear could move quite fast. The hunters were not catching up with her.

All summer the bear moved across the land of the stars while the hungry hunters followed. As autumn approached, some of them grew too weary to continue.

"I'm too far behind to catch up," said Saw-whet at the very end of the line. He was a clumsy owl and heavier than the others. Saw-whet dropped out of the chase first.

"Where's that lazy Saw-whet?" fretted Horned Owl, and he left to find his cousin.

Blue Jay tried to stay in the hunt, but by-and-by he and Pigeon lost their way and fell out of sight. That left only Robin, Chickadee with his pot, and Moose-bird to follow the trail of the bear.

At last, deep into autumn, the hunters overtook their prey. The cornered bear reared up on her hind legs and tried to defend herself. Growling and clawing she stood, but Robin shot her with his arrow. The bear fell over on her back, her blood coloring the leaves of autumn and staining Robin's breast a brilliant red.

All during the winter the dead bear lay on her back in the sky country. But that was not the end of the story. Her life spirit had entered another bear who had found its way to the den and was fast asleep. When spring awakens the sleeping earth, the den will reappear. A new star bear will come out of the den to search for berries in the sky, and Chickadee will begin the hunt again, as he does every year.

Moon and His Sister

Some of the greatest parties of all times were thrown by the Indians of the Northwest Coast. These tremendous give-away feasts were called potlatches. It was a contest to see which party would lavish the most food and the most extravagant gifts on its guests. A potlatch was an occasion for storytelling contests, too. Families had their own tales and sometimes acted them out with costumes and elaborate masks carved from wood. Moon masks were round and often decorated with pearly white shells. The Thompson River Indians who lived on the plateaus of south-central British Columbia shared the potlatch custom. They had a tale of a good-natured moon. Some families said his sister was a frog, others a rabbit. In this tale she is just a girl carrying water buckets.

MOON AND HIS SISTER

Small Star Near the Moon

The Moon was once a merry Indian whose face was even more brilliant than the Sun. He had one sister, a small star who could often be seen trailing along beside him, and countless star friends. One day, Moon called all of his friends together for a great feast. His small house was soon packed with guests.

When his sister arrived, Moon called for her to fetch water for him in her buckets. The task was not easy for deep winter was upon them, but the little sister went anyway. The cold wind howled. Ice had to be chipped from the water source, and the buckets were as heavy as great rocks.

When Moon's weary sister returned, there was hardly room in the crowded house for her to put down the buckets. She called to her brother. "Where can I sit?"

Moon's merry face burst into a grin. "There isn't space left for even a mouse in here," he laughed. "I guess you'll just have to sit on my head."

Moon's little sister was in no mood for his jokes. At once she jumped onto his head, and there she sits today with her water buckets. It is her shadow that dims his face.

Someday Moon hopes to shine as bright as the sun again. But he is a patient fellow. He enjoys smoking his pipe while he waits for his sister to move. On many nights cloud puffs from his pipe float about the sky.

Moon's star guests had such a good time at his party that they left the party in groups and danced their way across the sky. Most of them are there still, dancing and talking to one another.

The Boy Who Shot the Star to Find His Friend

The moon is a kind but powerful woman in many Native American Indian stories. In one tale she rescues a freezing girl from her cruel stepmother by helping her escape to the sky. But the Tlingits of the Alaskan panhandle told a story of an angry moon bent on revenge and of a star that promised help.

To many of the Northern tribes, the sky was like a roof through which the shining faces or homes of the star people would shine on those below. Some, like the Blackfoot Indians, thought stars were grandparents or relatives who had died but continued to love and be concerned for their earthly relatives.

THE BOY WHO SHOT THE STAR TO FIND HIS FRIEND

Star Near the Moon

A hunter's son and the son of a chief were once close friends. The boys played often on a hill beyond the village where they made arrows and practiced shooting them.

One night, as they climbed to the top of the hill, the hunter's son looked at the star-filled sky and remarked, "How small and weak the moon looks tonight." The chief's son warned him that he must not make the moon angry, but it was too late. The moon had heard the remark and was angry.

Suddenly a light like a rainbow surrounded the boys. When it disappeared, the chief's son was alone on the hill. He knew the angry moon had taken his friend.

The chief's son did not know what to do. He began shooting arrows, thinking he might try to hit the star closest to the moon. When he had used up all his arrows, he fell asleep, sad and exhausted.

The chief's son could not believe what he saw when he opened his eyes. There, hanging from the sky was a ladder of arrows! He had no idea what the ladder meant, but on the chance that it might have

11

something to do with the disappearance of his friend, the boy began to climb. The ladder took him beyond the bushes and treetops and into the clouds. He climbed for three days and nights. When he was hungry, he ate fruit from the twigs and branches caught in his hair. Reaching the top of the ladder at last, the boy fell asleep, exhausted again.

"Wake up! Wake up!" the boy heard through his sleep. "We know why you are here!" A young girl was shaking the shoulder of the chief's son. When he was awake, the girl led him to her grandmother's house. "We looked for you after your arrows hit our house," said the girl.

The grandmother welcomed the chief's son and told him that his friend was a captive in the moon's house next door. "We've heard him wailing for three days," she said. "We will do what we can to help you." With that, the old woman handed the boy three objects—a spruce cone, a rose branch, and a rock. "You will know when to make good use of these," she said.

The chief's son hurried to Moon's house and untied his friend. Climbing to the roof, he placed the spruce cone in the smoke hole of the house. "The wind will whistle through the cone and set up a wailing," whispered the boy to his friend. Then the two ran as fast as they could away from the Moon's house.

Moon wasn't fooled long by the howling cone. He came rolling after the boys faster than they could run. When Moon was at their heels, the chief's son tossed back the rose branch. It burst into a tangle of vines

and thorns. While the moon struggled to free himself, the boys ran ahead.

"You'll be sorry you tricked the moon!" roared Moon as he rumbled down upon them again. "I'll make you both prisoners!"

The chief's son looked over his shoulder and saw the moon reaching for him. He threw the rock. Crash! The rock became a mountain, and Moon ran right into it.

The boys puffed and panted back to the safety of the old grandmother's house. Now they wanted only to leave the sky country and go back home. The kind old grandmother knew what they were thinking. "Lie down here and rest," she told them. "Think of nothing but the hill where you played with your arrows. Everything will be as it should."

By now the boys knew how wise the old woman was, so they did exactly as she ordered. Curling up, they fell fast asleep at her feet.

When they awakened, the two friends found themselves lying on their grassy hilltop. Shaking sleep from their heads and twigs from their clothes, they walked back to their village. Their families, who had thought they would never see them again, held a great feast to celebrate their return.

Now when the two friends sit on their hill, they send thanks to the star next to the moon, for they know it is the small house of the grandmother who saved them from the angry moon.

The Dancing Braves

Pleiades is a small but brilliant cluster which seems to have seven stars. There are really many less visible stars in this shimmering constellation. It inspired tale-tellers across the continent. To some it was a swarm of bees. The Cherokees said Pleiades was seven boys who ran away from home. They were angry because their mothers gave them soup boiled from sticks and stones as punishment for not doing their work.

The Iroquois Indians, who lived in the woodlands of New York State, believed in witchcraft. Their tale about Pleiades has the spooky touch of curses and bewitchment.

THE DANCING BRAVES

Pleiades

Once long ago when summer was fading and the people of the tribe were building winter lodges, some of the younger boys played together near the edge of the woods. Too young to join the men hunting for winter meat, they pretended to be great warriors and danced the war dances.

One afternoon a strange old man appeared to the boys as they danced. He was dressed in a startling way. White feathers covered his robes, and his hair hung long and silver. Perhaps the stranger was one of the grandparents of the sky country. Perhaps he was only a confused old man. Whatever he may have been, his strong words were a warning to the boys that their wild dancing would come to no good. The boys paid no attention but went right on with their dances.

The next day they gathered again and danced until their shadows were longer than they were. Now the braves were hungry and tired but, when they thought of resting, they couldn't seem to stop. Their feet seemed to keep time to some mysterious beat that whirled and twirled them around their circle. Indeed, their feet seemed hardly to touch the ground. When they looked, the boys saw that they were rising in the air over rocks and bushes and trees.

Below, some of the tribe members saw the dancing braves. "Come back!" they pleaded.

"Stop dancing!" demanded the chief.

But still the boys rose dancing in the air.

The noise of the shouting reached the setting sun. He tried to stop the boys, but he had sunk too low in the heavens. The braves danced past, and the sun fell behind the hills.

Now Moon came up and wondered what the commotion was all about. The dancing braves shouted and whooped as they danced around her. "Stop!" she commanded in a voice that thundered.

"We cannot," cried the braves. So Moon invited them to join her legions of stars marching across the sky. Bouncing and whooping, the boys twirled into the procession, and soon all of the stars were whirling. The sky was in a flurry. Moon was alarmed.

"I must bring peace to the heavens and rest to these boys," Moon thought to herself. And after thinking a moment longer, Moon transformed the braves into a group of stars, placing them near the top of the sky.

Moon, in her wisdom, decided the boys should preside over the Indian New Year. Their path in the heavens brings them to stand each year directly over the Council House during the New Year's feast. Then, as Indians watch, the light of these small, bright stars sparkles and dances in the sky and everyone remembers the Dancing Braves.

The Maidens of the Northern Crown

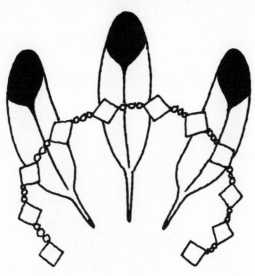

There is an incomplete circle of stars in the sky called the Northern Crown. Indian storytellers wondered why a star seemed to be missing. No one knows who told this story first, but the bittersweet tale was shared with different twists across the land. It came to be one of the most beloved of all Indian legends. Among the gentle hills and cool forests of the northern Great Lakes country, the Ojibwas told their version. The hunter heroes of their tales were able to change themselves into other forms as they wished, so this hunter became a mouse.

THE MAIDENS OF THE NORTHERN CROWN

Northern Crown

Once in a time long before this one, a young hunter returning to his village paused in a clearing. He had come upon a strange circle path. He searched but could find no path leading up to or away from the circle in the field. Shaking his head with bewilderment, he crouched down to wait and watch from the shadows of a birch grove. When night had fallen, the hunter heard strange music and noticed that a cluster of stars in the sky seemed to be traveling toward him. He clutched his arrows and caught his breath as the star cluster alighted in the clearing.

"I must be dreaming," murmured the hunter as he watched twelve beautiful maidens climb from a basket and begin to dance around the circle. They must have come here often, the hunter thought, because they wasted no time and seemed to know the place. When he had shaken the wonder from his head, the hunter stepped out of the shadows toward the dancing maidens. The music and the dancing stopped at once. Like birds seeking the safety of their nest, the maidens flew to their star basket. It rose at once into the night the way it had come.

21

The hunter, determined to find out what or whom he had seen, returned to the clearing on the following evening. Everything happened just as before. This time though, the hunter waited for a while and watched before cautiously letting himself be seen. The maidens ran from him again and disappeared into their basket. But the hunter had seen something that made him more determined than before. Among the maidens was one who was more graceful and, to the hunter's eyes, more beautiful than any of the others. "I must know this maiden," said the hunter to himself. And so he prepared to come again.

On the third night, the hunter changed himself into a mouse and hid in the grasses. The basket came down as it had before. This time, one dance flowed into the other, and the maidens stayed in the clearing until the stars had traveled from one horizon to the other.

Among the grass blades and stems, the mouse/hunter watched. And as he watched, he inched his way forward. It was the youngest dancing maid who had caught his eye, and now his heart pounded for her as he crept to her very feet. Suddenly then, the music came to an end and the maidens turned to their basket. Springing forward, the mouse/hunter became himself again and, with arms outreached, he grasped the youngest maid. The maidens cried out for their youngest sister, and she thrust her graceful body against the arms that held her fast. But the basket flew from the field and vanished.

Because he was kind and good, in time the hunter won the heart of the star maiden, and she became his wife. In a little more time, they had a son. As the child grew and the family worked and played together, the star woman was happy.

The hunter's wife was from the land of the star people, though, and could not live on earth forever. One night, while the hunter and his son slept, the eleven sisters came in their basket and carried the youngest sister off to the sky. The star people were pleased to have the circle of dancing sisters complete again, but they worried about the youngest sister, who never smiled. Although she loved her sisters, the hunter's wife was lonely and wept for her lost family.

At last the star people took pity on the youngest sister. They brought the hunter and his son to visit the star woman, but for only one night. "These are earth creatures," warned the father of the star people. "They must return or they will die."

"We will make the most of our time together," said the hunter's wife, and they did.

The star people watched the family and were moved. They wanted to help, so the father of the star people agreed to change the star wife, the hunter, and their son into three white falcons. Now the three belong to neither sky nor earth. They are free to visit both as they please. The remaining maidens of the Northern Crown dance together still. But it is said they will never leave the sky again.

The last star to disappear just before sunrise is the Morning Star. Although North American Indians did not know that this was really a planet and not a star, they did notice that it had no fixed position among the constellations. Their tales often made the roaming Morning Star a noble hunter. Morning Star and all the other star people were said to be super-human with powers only imagined by earthlings. The Blackfoot Indians allowed humans to marry stars in their tales. The lives of these humans were always tangled when they failed to understand the ways of the star people.

MORNING STAR TAKES A WIFE

Morning Star
Polaris

One hot summer night, when the world was young and strange things were possible, two maidens decided to sleep outside. As they drifted in and out of sleep, they watched the stars and, as maidens do, they dreamed about the husbands they might have one day. "I would have a hunter who keeps meat on the campfire and soft skins in our lodge," sighed one of the maids.

The other shook her head. "Whatever the wind brings me I would take if only he were bold in spirit." Then she pointed to the sky. "See that star there, the bright one? I want that one for a husband." Laughing, she rolled over, and they both fell asleep again.

The next day, as this impulsive maiden was gathering firewood in the forest, a handsome stranger came up to her. "I am the star man you wished for," he told the surprised young woman. "My name is Morning Star, and I have come for you."

The maiden took a half step away. She looked and thought, thought and looked. This handsome young man wore a generous robe of thick beaver skins and in his hair hung an eagle plume. "He has the walk of a

man of importance," observed the girl to herself. "Yet, there is a merry look in his eye." So with a toss of her head, she consented to go away with him.

"Look one last time down the footpath winding to your village," Morning Star said, pointing. "You cannot look back again." Morning Star watched as the maiden with a mind of her own gave but a glance over her shoulder. "Now you must shut your eyes," he commanded, placing an eagle plume in her hair, "and never look down." Then he took her boldly and led her to the sky. The laughter they shared fell like soft rain on the empty footpath.

Morning Star took his bride first to visit his mother, Moon, and his father, Sun. To welcome her to their lodge, Moon and Sun gave the young woman four berries and a few drops of water in a shell. Although she ate and ate, Morning Star's bride could not finish the berries or sip the last drop of water. There seemed always to be more. Then Moon offered another gift to Morning Star's bride with these words: "This," she said, "is a digger which you may use to dig roots for cooking any place in our land but one." Then

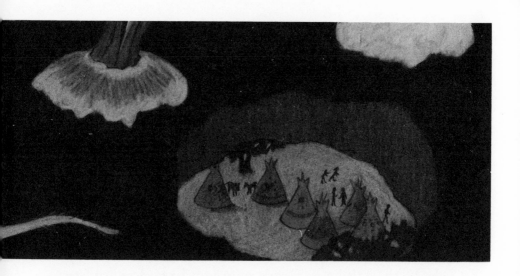

Moon pointed across the gardens of the sky to a large turnip. "That turnip is a sacred root to the sky people and must never be uprooted," she commanded.

"I will not fail to honor your turnip," promised the young woman as she hurried off with her handsome husband.

Morning Star and his bride were a contented pair, and in good time they had a child. In all the heavens there was nothing the star wife needed. Yet, although she was happy, she wondered about the sacred turnip. "Moon's rule is foolish," she thought. Her curiosity nagged at her as a fly nags on a hot summer day.

Finally, the nagging buzzed louder than the whisper of her pledge. "The sky country is full of turnips," she muttered to herself. "Who will know if I dig that one up?" So while her baby played near her, Morning Star's Wife dug up the forbidden root.

That evening, Moon shouted at Morning Star's door. "What have you done with the sacred turnip?" Moon demanded of the earthly wife. No truth could be hidden from Moon. Morning Star's Wife could only confess what she had done.

The lodge was darkly silent. "What did you see when you dug out the turnip?" asked Moon.

The wife of Morning Star replied, "I looked down through the hole and saw the earth, the trees, the rivers, and the lodges of my people."

Moon scowled. Sun's face clouded. The merry look faded from Morning Star's eyes. "I warned you never to look back," he said. "Now I cannot keep you with me any longer. You must take the boy with you and go back to your people."

Sun went to Spider to ask him to spin a strong web. In this, the star man's wife would be lowered to earth again. When Spider had done his work, Sun spoke again to the wife. "You have taken the law of the sky people carelessly," he frowned. "Now I have another rule you must follow." Then he told her she would be allowed to keep her son with her only if she followed his command. "When you reach the lodges of your people, you must not let the boy touch earth for fourteen days. If he does, he will be returned at once to the land of the stars," Sun said like a bear growls warning.

With Sun's words heavy in her thoughts, Morning Star's Wife was lowered with her child through the turnip hole to earth.

The people of Morning Star's Wife welcomed her back with a feast that lasted three days, for they had been sure she was dead. The woman ate and danced with the others, but she watched her small son every moment. Never would she let him slide to the ground as he begged. Never could he play in the dirt. Sun's warning echoed in her head!

"She loves her son more than life itself," whispered

the women of the village.

"She worries foolishly," scolded the star wife's old mother.

But one day Morning Star's Wife needed water for cooking. It was quiet in the lodge, and her son slept soundly on his bed. "What harm can come while my son sleeps so deeply?" thought Morning Star's Wife. "I will be out of the lodge and back again in the flash of a falling star." So, as she hurried off with her water bucket, she called to her mother, "Watch him carefully so that he stays on the bed!"

The old mother settled herself beside her grandson's bed, but soon the warmth of the darkened lodge closed around her. "My daughter worries foolishly," she muttered and allowed herself to fall asleep. Before long her rumbling snores had stirred the child beside her. He opened his eyes. He stretched his legs to the edge of the bed. Then he crawled down to play in the dirt, laughing to be free at last.

Like a leaf caught in the wind, when his toes grazed the earthen floor, the child rose to the top of the lodge. Out the smoke hole, above the trees he blew, over the hills and into the sky.

Slivers of baby laughter fell on the ears of the star wife returning with her water. Dropping the bucket, she flew into the lodge, shouting her son's name. But the bed and the room stood empty of her small son's form.

That night, wrapped in her sadness, Morning Star's Wife lay under clear skies searching the heavens for some sign of her lost child. Her eyes swept and swept again the farthest reaches of the sky and, when her head ached from the watching, she was sure she saw something different. A new star gleamed where the empty turnip hole had once been. Morning Star's Wife kept her eyes on the star all night. She watched it the next night and the next. This star seemed easy to find. It kept its place always in the sky while the other stars revolved around it. In time Morning Star's Wife looked upon this star as her own.

Among the people of Morning Star's Wife, her star became known as the Fixed Star. They used it to help them tell direction. They looked for it to help them chart the heavens. But to Morning Star's Wife, the Fixed Star brought a special comfort. When she was lonely, she could always find her son. She knew he would look down on her always from his place above.

ONE LAST WORD FROM THE STARS

On warm summer nights when the sky is like dark glass and the stars stand clear enough to count, beware! The Sioux warned against trying to count the stars. It was believed that if you dared to look at the sky and count even "one" mentally, you might be doomed. They thought death was certain if the counting was begun but not finished.

WHERE THE TALES BEGAN

1. *THE NEVER-ENDING BEAR HUNT* was carefully recorded with drawings by Stansbury Hagar in 1900.

2. *MOON AND HIS SISTER* is based on variants of a widely told tale.

3. *THE BOY WHO SHOT THE STAR TO FIND HIS FRIEND* has been passed to us by the Tlinget peoples. John R. Swanton wrote it down in 1909.

4. *THE DANCING BRAVES* is retold from several versions. One was reported by Wm. M. Beauchamp in 1900.

5. *THE MAIDENS OF THE NORTHERN CROWN* is an old tale with many versions. Henry R. Schoolcraft wrote his in 1860.

6. *MORNING STAR TAKES A WIFE* was adapted from parts of a Blackfeet legend told to Clark Wissler by Wolf-Head, who died in 1905.

The designs and illustrations for this book were carefully researched for each tribe represented, largely through the resources of the Milwaukee Public Museum.

GLOSSARY

Alaskan panhandle—the southward extending Pacific coastline of the state of Alaska

Antelope—the mammal known in North America as the antelope is actually the pronghorn, and is the swiftest of all North American mammals

Arrow shaft—the long stem to which the head and feathers of an arrow are attached

Auriga—constellation also called "The Charioteer", located between Perseus and Gemini

Ax—handled tool with a sharpened end used for chopping

Beaver—a large rodent with a broad, flat tail. With its long front teeth, the beaver cuts trees which it uses to build dams and dens along streams.

Betelgeuse—a very bright star of the first magnitude seen near one shoulder of Orion, the constellation also called "The Hunter"

Big Dipper—the seven most obvious stars (which resemble a dipper) in the constellation Ursa Major or Big Bear.

Big Horn—a wild sheep. The males have large curling horns.

Birchbark boxes—lidded containers made by lacing together strips of bark from the birch tree

Boötes—also known as "The Herdsman." The handle of the Big Dipper points to this constellation.

Camas root—the edible bulb of the camas plant, a member of the lily family

Canoe—a long, narrow boat made of wood, bark or hides. Canoes made from birchbark were lightweight and easy for one or a few to carry. Some dugout canoes, made from huge logs, could carry more than fifty people. These were often decorated.

Caribou—a member of the deer family living in northern forests and bogs. Unlike other deer, both males and females have antlers.

Cassiopeia's Chair—a W-shaped constellation located between Andromeda and Cepheus

Chickadee—a small, lively bird with grey back and wings

Chinook wind—along the Pacific coast this is a warm wind which comes from the southwest. When it blows down the mountains in winter and early spring, it often melts snow at the base of the slopes.

Clearing—an area without trees

Constellation—a group of stars which appear to resemble a person or object

Corona Borealis—also known as the Northern Crown, a small constellation which seems to be a broken circle, between Hercules and Boötes

Council house—meeting place for the tribal council

Coyote—a swift, cunning mammal related to, but smaller than, the wolf. There are many American Indian tales about Coyote.

Eagle plume—a cluster of feathers worn as an ornament

Elk—the largest member of the deer family. Older males have large, many-tinted antlers.

Fir—an evergreen of the pine family

Fisher—a dark brown forest mammal related to weasels. Fishers are fierce hunters.

Fixed Star—also known as Polaris or The North Star

Fox—a sly, cunning mammal of the dog family having a bushy tail

Good medicine—helpful spiritual powers

Grazing—to feed on the vegetation

Great White River in the Sky—the name given by some Native Americans to the Milky Way

Grizzly Bear—a large and powerful bear of a brownish-yellow color

Guardian spirit—a supernatural being that was a personal spiritual helper and the source of a man's or a woman's power

High Plateau Country of Oregon—the Columbia plateau covering most of eastern Oregon. Much of this area is rugged and mountainous.

Horizon—the place where earth and sky seem to meet

Horned Owl—a large owl with tufts of feathers resembling horns on either side of its head

Labrador—a large peninsula in northeastern Canada bordered by Hudson Bay and the Atlantic Ocean

Ladle—a utensil used for dipping up liquid

Leech—a segmented worm which usually feeds on blood. Most live in water.

Migrations—the regular journey from one region to another for feeding and breeding

Milky Way—seen as a broad, irregular band of light stretching across the night sky, it is actually the light of billions of stars in our own galaxy

Morning Star—the last star visible in the sky after daybreak. The Morning Star is a planet, not a real star (usually the planet Venus.) Some ancients said Morning Star was a hunter among the sky people.

Mosquitoes—small insects with long legs. The female feeds on the blood of mammals.

Muskrat—mammal about the size of a small house cat which has dense dark brown fur and lives along streams and rivers. Water vegetation is its main food and the building material for its houses.

North Star—also known as *Polaris*. This is the star in the Northern Hemisphere toward which the axis of the earth points. As a result, when we look at the sky, all of the stars seem to circle around this star.

Northwest Coast—an area of the North American Pacific Coast extending northward from Northern California to Alaska

Nova Scotia—includes a peninsula of the Canadian mainland as well as Cape Breton Island and extends into the Atlantic Ocean northeast of Maine

Olympic Peninsula of Washington—a rugged mountain region in the northwest corner of Washington State bordered by the Strait of Juan de Fuca on the north and the Pacific Ocean on the west

Orion—a constellation that represents a hunter with a belt and sword. It is a winter constellation and has more bright stars than any other.

Perseus—a constellation located between Taurus ("The Bull") and Cassiopeia

Planet—one of the large heavenly bodies which revolve around our sun. At night planets reflect the light of our sun and look like stars, but are not. Ancient people noticed that the planets moved on their own individual paths across the heavens.

Pleiades—a bright cluster of stars in the constellation Taurus or "The Bull." Six or seven of the stars are visible to the average eye.

Polaris—another name for the North Star

Potlatch—at these lavish feasts, the host gave away valuable gifts to guests

Prairie—mostly level, grass-covered plains

Puget Sound—a huge bay between the Olympic Peninsula and the Cascade Mountains in Washington State. It is connected to the Pacific Ocean by the Strait of Juan de Fuca.

Robin—a migratory bird commonly known for its red breast

Salmon—a fish. The Pacific Salmon is known for the long journeys it makes upstream to its breeding grounds.

Saw-whet—a small owl with a harsh voice

Skunk—a cat-sized animal which sprays a foul smelling scent when threatened

Smoke hole—an opening constructed in houses, tipis, and lodges so that smoke from the fire could escape

Snow goose—a large bird which breeds in the Artic tundra and winters in more southern marshes

Spruce—an evergreen pine tree

Spruce cone—the pinecone from a spruce tree

Star—a shining heavenly body visible in the sky at night. Our sun is a star.

Sturgeon glue—glue made by cooking the heads, bones, and scales of a fish until a gelatin is formed

Trickster—someone who fools others

Turnip—a vegetable with edible leaves and root

Warrior—a person experienced in fighting wars

Water buckets—containers usually made from carved wood, woven plant material, or tightly sealed birchbark

White falcon—a magnificent long-winged bird

Yew—an evergreen tree or bush